Three Rolls and One Doughnut

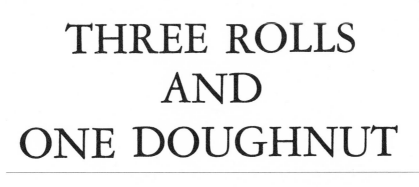

THREE ROLLS AND ONE DOUGHNUT

Fables from Russia retold by
Mirra Ginsburg

pictures by Anita Lobel

6828

THE DIAL PRESS · NEW YORK

❀ Editor's Note ❀

Russia is an enormous country inhabited by many peoples with vastly different cultures. The folk tales, fables, and riddles in this collection come from all parts of the country, east and west, north and south. Here are Russian tales, Latvian tales, Kalmuck, Armenian, Ukrainian, Kazakh, and Jewish tales. Some of them have spread across the land and are known to children—and to adults—everywhere. Others belong more specifically to one people or to a group of neighboring peoples. Still others are told in different versions in different parts of the country. And some are even imported from abroad and altered in the process to reflect local conditions and the local character.

But whatever shape they take in the telling, they are all a part of the universal heritage of folk culture, a distillation of the wit and wisdom that lies at the heart of man's experience of himself and the world he lives in.

With but a few exceptions, these tales appear in English for the first time. I have gathered them here in the hope that American readers will find them as delightful as have the many generations in Russia that have told and listened to them for centuries past.

 Contents

Three Rolls and One Doughnut

✿ Rabbit Fat ✿

Poor Stepan drove rich Ivan to the city. A rabbit jumped out of the bushes by the roadside and hopped away. Rich Ivan said to poor Stepan, "In our woods there are rabbits five times the size of this. One day I went out hunting and killed three dozen in a row. One was as big as a ram. I skinned him, and, do you know, he had twenty pounds of fat on him. That's the kind of rabbits we have."

Stepan listened and listened. Then he said to his horse, "Steady, Old Gray, we're coming to the bridge that breaks down under liars."

Rich Ivan heard this and said, "There are rabbits and rabbits. Well, maybe it wasn't all of twenty pounds, but it was at least ten."

"Sure," said Stepan, "a rabbit like all rabbits."

They drove on, and then Ivan asked Stepan, "How soon do we come to the bridge you spoke of?"

"Soon, soon."

"Well, Stepan," said Ivan. "Maybe that rabbit did not have ten pounds of fat, just three or four."

"All right," said Stepan. "Four is four."

They drove some more. Ivan began to sigh and fidget in his seat, and then he asked again, "How soon do we come to that bridge, Stepan?"

"Soon, soon. It's just down that hill."

"Hm," said Ivan. "Well, you know, Stepan, the rabbit really had no fat at all. Who ever heard of fat rabbits, anyway?"

"Sure enough," said Stepan. "A rabbit like all rabbits."

They drove down the hill, and Ivan asked, "And where's the bridge you spoke of, Stepan?"

"Why, it melted," said Stepan. "It melted away like the fat on your rabbit."

❀ How the Peasant Helped His Horse ❀

A peasant drove to market to sell his grain. The roads were bad, and his horse got tired pulling the heavy load. The peasant saw that the horse could not go much farther. He took one of the bags of grain from the cart, put it across his shoulders, climbed back into the driver's seat, and said to the horse, "Giddy-up, giddy-up! It's easier for you now! I am carrying a whole bag on my own shoulders!"

❀ Three Rolls and One Doughnut ❀

A peasant walked a long way from his village to the city. By the time he got there, he was very hungry. He bought a roll and ate it, but he was still hungry. He bought another roll and ate it, but he was still hungry. He bought a third roll and ate it. He was still hungry. Then he bought a doughnut. He ate it— and what do you think?—he was not hungry any more.

"Ah!" He clapped himself on the forehead. "What a fool I was to have wasted all that good money on rolls! I should have bought a doughnut to begin with!"

❀ How the Peasant Divided the Geese ❀

There were two neighbors who lived in a village. One was rich and greedy. The other was poor. The rich man's house was full of goods. The poor man had a wife and many children but little food. And all he owned in the world was a single goose. Things went from bad to worse. The children were hungry. One day the peasant killed the goose and told his wife to roast it. It would have made a fine dinner for them, but they had no bread to eat it with. And what's the good of meat without bread?

So the peasant said to his wife, "We cannot live without bread. I'll take the goose to the lord and see if he will give me some flour."

And his wife said, "Go, husband."

The peasant came to the lord: "I brought you a present, the best thing I have. If it pleases you, perhaps you will give me some bread."

"Thank you, my good man! This is indeed a fine present. But now you must divide the goose among us so that everybody gets a fair share. If you do, I will reward you. If you don't, you'll get a thrashing."

The peasant asked for a knife and began to carve the goose. He cut off the head and gave it to the lord: "You are the head of the family. You get the head."

He cut off the rump and gave it to the lady: "You sit at

8

home and look after the house. The rump is for you."

He cut off the feet and gave them to the sons: "You get the feet, to walk up and down the paths and keep your father's garden neat."

The daughters got the wings: "You will not stay with your parents long. You'll grow up and fly away to sing your own song."

The rest of the goose he took for himself: "I am only a foolish, simple peasant. I'll eat the headless body of the present."

The lord laughed. He gave the peasant a glass of wine, a bag of flour, and sent him home.

When the rich, greedy peasant heard about it, he told his wife to roast five fat geese and took them to the lord.

"What do you want, peasant?" asked the lord.

"I brought you a little present. Five geese. The best of my flock."

"Thank you, my good man! And now you must divide the geese among us so that everybody gets a fair share. If you do, I will reward you. If you don't, you'll get a thrashing."

The rich peasant hemmed and hawed and scratched his head. But try as he might, he could not think of how to make a fair division.

Then the lord sent for the poor peasant and told him to divide the geese. The peasant took one goose and gave it to the lord and the lady, saying, "Now you are three!"

He gave another goose to the sons, saying, "Now you are three!"

He gave the third goose to the daughters, and said, "Now you are three!"

And he took the two remaining geese for himself: "Now we are three!"

The lord laughed again and said to the poor peasant, "I see you are a clever man! You made a fair division and got yourself a share as well."

Then he gave him a glass of wine and a whole wagonload of flour. But the greedy, rich peasant was sent to the stable, where he got the thrashing of his life.

❀ Which Eye Is Blind ❀

A man's horse was stolen from the stable. When the man discovered his loss, he ran to the market and soon found the thief trying to sell the horse. He caught it by the mane and asked, "Whose horse is this?"

"Mine," said the thief.

The owner covered the horse's eyes with his hand and said, "If it's yours, tell me which of its eyes is blind!"

The thief had not taken a good look at the horse, and he tried to guess: "The left."

The owner moved his hand from the left eye.

"No," cried the frightened thief. "I made a mistake, it is the right."

The owner took away his hand and everybody saw that neither of the eyes was blind.

And so the clever owner got his horse back. And the thief got twenty lashes and was driven out of town.

The Best Liar

Once upon a time there lived a king who was very, very bored. To amuse himself he sent out criers to every town and village in his land to find the best liar.

"Hear ye, hear ye!" shouted the criers. "The king will give a golden apple to the man who tells him the biggest lie!"

People began to come to the king from all ends of the land; princes, merchants, officials. But nobody could please the king.

At last a poor shepherd came to the palace with a large pot in his hands.

"What do you want?" asked the king.

"Good morning, your Majesty," said the shepherd. "I've come for my money. You owe me a potful of gold."

"A potful of gold?" cried the king. "Ridiculous. I do not owe you anything!"

"Oh, yes, you do. I lent it to you last year."

"Liar! This is the biggest lie I've ever heard!"

"It is? Then give me the golden apple."

The king saw that the shepherd had tricked him.

"Well, it is not really a lie."

"It isn't? Then pay your debt!"

The king had to admit that the shepherd had won. He gave him the golden apple and sent him home in peace.

❀ The Traveler's Tale ❀

A traveler was riding through the woods and lost his way. All day he circled around and around, and in the evening he came to a house. He knocked at the door and asked, "Good people, will you give me shelter for the night?"

The master of the house said, "You are welcome, but on one condition. You must tell us stories the whole night through."

The traveler rested a little and warmed himself by the fire. Then the family gathered to hear his tales.

"Before I start," said the traveler, "I will tell you *my* condition. Nobody must interrupt me. If I am interrupted, I'll tell no more stories and will go to sleep."

Everybody agreed, and the traveler began, "One day I was walking through the forest. It was a vast forest, and so dense that you could barely make your way among the trees. Suddenly a crow flew out of a tree. Yes, a crow, a black crow, a crow like all crows. And the crow flew and flew, and would not sit down. It flew over one tree, then under another, then between two trees. And it flew, and flew, and flew, that black, black crow, and . . ."

"And then?" someone asked.

"And then you interrupted me, and so I will not tell you any more," said the traveler. He lay down on the bench near the warm stove and had a good night's sleep.

❁ The Lost Penny ❁

"Boo-hoo . . ."

"Why are you crying, little boy?"

"Boo-hoo . . . I had a penny and I lost it."

"Here is a penny. Don't cry."

"Thank you-oo . . . Boo-hoo . . ."

"You have a penny. Why are you crying now?"

"If I hadn't lost mine, I'd have two."

🌸 The Golden Key 🌸

On a cold winter day a woodcutter went to the forest for some firewood. By the time he got there he was chilled to the bone.

"Let me dig up the snow," he said. "I'll find some twigs and make a fire. After I warm up I'll go to work."

He cleared away some snow, and—what do you think?—he saw a little golden casket.

"Wait," he said to himself. "Where there's a casket there must also be a key!"

He dug and dug and found the key. And now he will open the golden casket with the golden key and look inside.

You want to know what's in it? Wait a while. As soon as he opens it we'll find out.

🌼 Pete 🌼

"Pete, go thresh some wheat!"
"I can't. I have a stomachache."
"Pete, come and eat!"
"Where's my big spoon?"

🌼 The Hole 🌼

"Fedul, why so sad?"
"I burned a hole in my coat."
"You can mend it."
"I have no needle."
"How big is the hole?"
"There's nothing left but the collar."

❋ Two Friends ❋

Two boys lived in a village. One was called Dychak, the other Kechak. They were great friends and were always together.

Dychak boasted that his father was the bravest man alive, and that he was just like his father. Kechak could safely go with him to the darkest, deepest forest.

Kechak listened and believed him.

One day they went for a walk in the woods and met a bear. The bear rose on his hind feet and growled.

Dychak dashed to the nearest tree and climbed up to the very top as fast as he could.

The bear wanted to jump on Kechak, but the boy dropped to the ground and pretended to be dead.

The bear walked over and sniffed him, but Kechak did not move. After a while the bear decided that he must be dead and went away.

Dychak climbed down the tree and asked his friend, "Was the bear talking to you?"

"He was," said Kechak.

"What did he say?"

"He said, 'Never go to the woods with friends who climb trees better than squirrels.'"

✹ The Bubble, the Straw, and the Shoe ✹

In a certain village, there lived a bubble, a straw, and a shoe. One day they went to the forest to chop some firewood. They came to a river and did not know how to cross it. The shoe said to the bubble, "You can float. We'll use you as a boat."

But the bubble said, "No, shoe. Let the straw lie down from bank to bank, and we will walk across it."

The straw stretched out across the river.

The shoe began to walk across. But the straw broke, and they both fell into the water and drowned.

And the bubble laughed, and laughed, and laughed until it burst.

✾ Take Four from Four ✾

A teacher asked a boy, "What will be left if you take four from four?"

The boy thought and thought and could not answer.

"Let's try an example," said the teacher. "Suppose you have four pennies in your pocket and they drop out. What will be left in your pocket?"

"A hole," said the boy.

❁ Hatchet Gruel ❁

A soldier was going home on leave. He walked and walked till he got tired and hungry. He came to a village and knocked at the first house: "Let me come in and take a rest, good people!"

An old woman opened the door: "Come in, soldier, come in."

"And do you have a bite of food for me, good woman?"

The old woman was rich but stingy. She was so stingy that she would not give you a piece of ice in winter.

"Ah, my man, I have not eaten anything myself today. I don't have a crumb in the house."

"Well, if you don't, you don't," said the soldier.

Then he noticed a hatchet without a handle under the bench.

"If you have nothing else, we can make a nice gruel out of the hatchet."

The old woman clapped her hands: "Gruel? Out of the hatchet? How can you do that?"

"Give me a pot. I'll show you how to make gruel out of a hatchet."

The old woman brought a large pot. The soldier washed the hatchet, put it into the pot, poured in water, and put the pot on the fire.

The old woman watched.

The soldier took a spoon and stirred the gruel. Then he tasted it.

25

"Well, how is it?" asked the woman.

"Almost ready," said the soldier. "A pity there is no salt."

"Oh, I have salt. Here, put some in."

The soldier salted his gruel and tasted it again: "It would be nice if we could add a handful of oats!"

The old woman brought a cup of oats from the cellar.

The soldier poured the oats into the gruel and went on stirring it.

The woman watched and wondered.

"M-m, what a tasty gruel," said the soldier. "All it needs is a spoonful of butter. Then it would be perfect."

The old woman brought some butter, too, and they put it into the gruel.

"Now take a spoon, my good woman."

They sat down to eat the gruel, and with every spoonful they said, "Good!"

"I never thought you could make such a fine gruel out of a hatchet!" the old woman marveled.

And the soldier ate and grinned into his whiskers.

The Peasant and the Bear

One fine spring day a peasant went out into the field to plant turnips. He plowed and he sowed. Suddenly a bear came out of the woods.

"Go away, peasant, or I'll break your bones."

"Don't break my bones, Teddy dear. It would be much better for us to plant turnips together. I'll take only the roots, and you can have the tops."

"Good," said the bear. "But if you fool me, don't let me catch you in my woods." And he went back into the woods.

The turnips grew big and strong. In the fall the peasant came to dig them up, and the bear came out for his share.

"Hello, Teddy bear, here is your share. You get the tops, I get the roots."

The peasant gave the bear all the leaves and piled the turnips into his cart. The next day he took them to market to sell. On the road he met the bear.

"Where are you going, peasant?"

"To town, to sell the roots."

"Give me one. I want to taste it. I want to see what the roots are like."

The peasant gave him a turnip and the bear bit into it.

"Oh-h," he roared. "You fooled me! Your roots are sweet. Don't let me catch you in the woods now. I'll break your bones."

The next year the peasant planted wheat in the same field. He came to reap, and the bear was there, waiting for his share.

"You won't fool me this time, peasant. Give me my share!"

"Have it your way," said the peasant. "You can have the roots, and I'll take the tops."

They gathered the wheat. The peasant gave the bear the roots and piled the wheat into his cart to take home.

The bear tried and tried, but could do nothing with the roots.

He got angry at the peasant, and ever since that day the bear and the peasant are enemies.

❀ Plans ❀

A poor peasant was crossing a field and saw a hare under a bush. "What luck!" he said to himself. "Now I'll get rich and live like a lord! I'll catch the hare and sell it in the market. Then I'll buy a pig. The pig will bear a dozen piglets. The piglets will grow up, and each will bear a dozen more. I'll sell them and build a house with the money. Then I'll get married, and my wife will bear two sons—Vaska and Vanka. The boys will plow the field, and I'll sit by the window and give orders."

"Hey, boys, you lazybones! Get to work! Quit fooling!" the peasant shouted.

The hare got frightened and ran away.

And that was the end of the house, and the land, and the wife, and the sons.

❀ Riddles ❀

Who goes dressed in summer
And naked in winter?

Four brothers
Under one roof.

It's not a bush, but it has leaves,
It's not a shirt, but it is sewn,
It's not a slave, but it is bound,
It's not a man, but it tells a story.

He wears a wooden shirt,
And his nose is dark.
Wherever he goes,
He leaves a mark.

When they are empty, they stand,
When they are full, they walk.

🏵 A Thousand Thoughts 🏵

A hunter dug a pit in the woods, covered it with twigs, and waited. What beast would fall into his trap?

A fox ran through the woods. She kept looking up at the birds in the trees and—plop—into the pit!

A crane flew over and came down to look for food. His feet got tangled in the twigs. He began to struggle and—plop—into the pit!

Now the fox is in trouble, and the crane is in trouble. They don't know what to do, how to get out of the pit.

The fox runs around and around, raising clouds of dust. And the crane stands on one foot and does not move from the spot. All he does is peck the earth before him. Peck-peck, peck-peck!

Both are thinking hard: How can they get out of the pit?

The fox runs and runs: "I have a thousand, thousand, thousand thoughts!"

And the crane pecks and pecks: "And I have only one thought!"

"What a fool," thinks the fox. "All he does is peck. Doesn't he know the earth is big and you cannot peck through it?"

And she goes on circling and circling around the pit: "I have a thousand, thousand, thousand thoughts!"

And the crane keeps pecking: "And I have only one thought!"

The hunter went out to see if anyone had fallen into his trap.

When the fox heard him coming, she ran still faster, around

and around the pit. "I have a thousand, thousand, thousand thoughts!"

And the crane kept quiet and stopped pecking altogether. The fox looked over. The crane was lying on his side, his legs stretched out. He died of fright, the poor thing!

The hunter lifted up the twigs and saw the fox and the crane. The fox ran around the pit, and the crane lay still and did not breathe.

"You good for nothing fox," cried the hunter. "Killed such a fine bird!"

He pulled the crane out by his legs and felt him. Still warm! And the hunter got even angrier at the fox.

And the fox ran around and around the pit, and didn't know what thought to follow. She had a thousand, thousand, thousand thoughts!

"You wait!" said the hunter. "Wait and see what you'll get for killing the crane!"

He put the bird down by the pit and turned to the fox.

The moment he turned, the crane spread out his wings and cried, "I had one single thought!"

And he was gone.

And the fox with her thousand, thousand, thousand thoughts ended up as a collar on a coat.

🏵 The Lion, the Fish, and the Man 🏵

One day a lion was talking to a fish in the river. A man was passing by, and he stopped to listen.

The fish saw the man and flicked his tail and slipped away to the bottom.

When they met again, the lion asked the fish, "Why did you slip away?"

"I saw a man."

"What about it?"

"Man is cunning and dangerous. It's best to stay away from him."

"What kind of beast is this man?" asked the lion. "Just let me find him. I'll eat him up."

And the lion went off to look for a man.

Down the road he met a little boy.

"Are you a man?" asked the lion.

"No, not yet. I am a boy. I will not be a man for a long time yet."

The lion did not touch him and went on.

Then he met an old man, hobbling with a stick.

"Are you a man?" asked the lion.

"Oh, no, my friend! What kind of a man am I now? I was a man once upon a time."

The lion did not touch him either.

"Strange," said the lion. "It seems impossible to find a man anywhere!"

He walked and he walked until he met a soldier with a gun and a saber.

"Are you a man?" asked the lion.

"I am," said the soldier.

"Well, then, I'll eat you up!"

"Wait a while," said the soldier. "I'll make it easier for you. Get back a little, and I'll jump into your mouth myself. Open it, wider!"

The lion backed away and opened his mouth as wide as he could. The soldier raised his gun, and—BOOM!—the bullet whizzed over the lion's head, just barely missing it. Then the soldier ran up to the lion and lopped off an ear with his saber.

The lion turned and ran for dear life. When he came to the river, the fish swam up and asked, "Well, did you find a man?"

"Oh," said the lion, "you were right. Man is cunning and dangerous! It took me a long time to find him. One creature said he used to be a man, another said he was waiting to become one. And when I found a man, I surely wished I hadn't. He told me to back up and he would jump into my mouth. Then he stretched out his paw and there was thunder, and the lightning almost struck me down. And then he ran up to me, stuck out his tongue, and licked my ear off! It's still bleeding."

"You see?" said the fish. "I told you! Next time you will stay away from man."

❀ The Cat and the Tiger ❀

A cat went walking in the woods and came upon a dead tigress. A little tiger cub sat whimpering near his mother. The cat took pity on the orphan. She brought him home and nursed him with her own milk. In time, the cub grew big and strong and began to hunt for his own food. But one day he could not find anything to eat. He was very hungry, and he prepared to pounce on the cat, intending to make a meal of her. The cat, however, guessed his plan. She dashed away and quickly scrambled up a tree.

The tiger ran up to the tree and said plaintively, "My dear, dear nurse! You brought me up on your own milk, and I love you as my own mother. You taught me everything I know. Why didn't you teach me to climb trees as well?"

"Ah," said the cat. "I saved that for myself." And she climbed still higher.

❁ Two Stubborn Goats ❁

Two goats met on a narrow bridge high over a brook.

"Step back!" cried one. "I have to cross!"

"You step back!" cried the other. "I have to cross!"

"No, you step back!"

And the two stubborn goats bumped heads and locked horns, each trying to push the other back. They pushed and pushed, and—plop! Both landed in the brook below.

They clambered out of the water and limped away, groaning, muddy, and bruised. And each one still insists that it was the other's fault.

❁ The Jolly Sparrow ❁

From branch to branch, from tree to bush—hop, skip, hop, skip—all day long goes the sparrow.

"Cheep-cheep! Cheep-cheep!" from morning till night. He is never worried, never sad. He finds a crumb here, a worm there, and that is all he needs to keep him bright and merry.

And the old black crow sits on a tree, puffed up with self-importance. She hates everyone, and nothing pleases her. She looks at the sparrow out of the corner of her eye and envies his happiness. "Cheep-cheep!" he sings all day long. Hop, skip! Stupid sparrow! She'll put some sense into his head.

"Tell me, sparrow," asks the crow. "How do you keep alive? Where do you get your food?"

The sparrow cannot sit still for a moment. He flits from place to place and says, "There is food all around. Here a grain, there a crumb. Delicious."

"And what if you choke on something? Then you'll die?"

"Cheep," says the sparrow. "Why die? I'll scratch inside my mouth and get it out."

"And what if the scratches bleed?"

"I'll drink some water and the blood will stop."

"And what if you get your feet wet and catch a cold?"

"Cheep-cheep! I'll make a fire and get warm; then I'll be well again."

"And what if the fire spreads?"

"I'll flutter my wings and put it out."

"And what if you burn your wings and cannot fly?"

"I'll ask the doctor to cure me."

"And what if you don't find a doctor?"

"Cheep-cheep! I'll find a grain here, a worm there, a soft place for my nest. The kindly sun will warm me. The breeze will cool me. And I'll get well without a doctor!" says the sparrow merrily. "Cheep!"—and away he goes.

And the old crow ruffles her feathers, closes her eyes, buries her beak in her chest, and thinks, "That stupid sparrow! Only fools don't worry about tomorrow."

✿ The Valiant Lion ✿

A rabbit hopping in the field wanted a drink. He looked around and saw a well. He went up to the well, bent over it, and jumped away. Then he turned and dashed off for dear life, forgetting all about his thirst.

"Where are you running?" the fox called out to him.

"I am escaping from a terrible beast. His face is crooked, his ears are long, he has huge whiskers, and he's about to jump out and come after me."

The fox got frightened and they ran together.

They ran and ran without a backward glance until they met a bear.

"Hey, wait a minute! What happened?" cried the bear.

They told the bear about the beast, and he ran with them. On the way they met all sorts of animals, big and small, and each one joined in the flight. And they would still be running if they had not met a lion. The animals stopped short at the sight of the lion, afraid to take another step forward or back.

"What's going on here?" roared the lion.

They told him breathlessly about the monster in the well, each vying with the other in describing the terrors of the beast.

The lion said, "I won't believe it until I see it myself."

The animals begged him not to go to what would surely be his death.

"Cowards!" the lion growled, and commanded them to follow him.

The animals trembled with fear. It was too terrifying to turn back, and it was too dangerous to provoke the lion. What could they do?

Reluctantly they followed him, huddling together for safety. When they came to the well, the lion said contemptuously, "Well, where's your monster? Let us see him! Come out, come out, whatever you are!"

Then he turned to the shivering animals: "You silly cowards! If there were a monster in the well, he would have jumped out and attacked you long ago."

The animals took courage, and the lion approached the well, looked down, and roared in anger.

The animals backed away. And the lion saw a shaggy monster with a frightful face and blazing eyes looking at him from the well, ready to pounce.

The lion's roars grew louder and louder. But the beast in the well roared back and would not retreat.

The animals stood frozen with terror.

The lion lashed his tail over his flanks, dug the earth with his paws, and shook his mane.

But the monster in the well seemed to mock him, repeating every movement he made.

The proud lion could endure it no longer. He leaped into the well to meet his adversary. There was a great big splash, and that was the end of the lion.

🏵 The Fox and the Thrush 🏵

A hungry fox saw a thrush sitting high in a tree.

"Good morning, dear thrush," said the fox. "I heard your pleasant voice, and it made my heart rejoice."

"Thanks for your kindness," said the thrush.

The fox called out, "What did you say? I cannot hear you now. Why don't you come down on the grass? We'll take a nice, long walk and have a good, friendly talk."

But the thrush said, "It isn't safe for us birds on the grass."

"You are not afraid of me?" cried the fox.

"Well, if not you, then some other animal."

"Oh, no, my dearest friend. There is a new law in the land. Today there is peace among all beasts. We are all brothers. None is allowed to hurt another."

"That's good," said the thrush. "I see dogs coming this way. Under the old law, you would have had to run away. But now there is no reason for you to be frightened."

As soon as the fox heard about the dogs, he pricked up his ears and started running.

"Where are you going?" cried the thrush. "We have a new law in the land. The dogs won't touch you now."

"Who knows," answered the fox as he ran. "Perhaps they have not heard about it yet."

❀ The Snake and the Fish ❀

A snake and a fish became fast friends.

"Sister dear," said the snake to the fish. "Take me on your back and give me a ride in the sea."

"Very well," said the fish. "Sit down on my back and I'll take you for a ride. You will see what our sea is like."

The snake coiled herself around the fish, and they swam out to sea. They had not gone too far when the snake bit the fish.

"Sister dear," asked the fish, "why do you bite me?"

"It was an accident," said the snake.

They went on, and the snake bit the fish a second time.

"Sister dear, why do you bite me?" asked the fish.

"I didn't mean to; the sun made me dizzy," said the snake.

They went on further, and the snake bit the fish a third time.

"Sister dear, why do you keep biting me?"

"That's my way," said the snake.

"Well, I have a way too," said the fish and dived into the sea.

The snake got her lungs full of water and never saw the light of day again.

🏵 The Braggart 🏵

There was a rabbit in the woods who liked to brag: "I am the bravest beast of all!" he would say. "I have huge paws, huge whiskers, and huge teeth. I'm not afraid of anybody."

When the crow heard about it, she went to look for the braggart. She found him hiding under a bush.

"I won't brag any more, Auntie Crow!" he cried.

"And what did you say before?" she asked.

"I said I am the bravest beast of all. I said I have huge paws, huge whiskers, and huge teeth. I said I'm not afraid of anybody."

She picked him up by the ear and shook him. "Don't brag any more! Don't brag any more!" And she flew up and settled on the bush.

At that moment a dog was passing by. He jumped up and caught the crow. The rabbit was so terrified that he forgot all caution. He left his hiding place and bounded down the hill.

At the sight of the rabbit the dog let the crow go and dashed after him. The crow flew up into a tree, and the rabbit escaped into his burrow.

The next day the crow and the rabbit met again.

"Forgive me," she said. "I see now that you spoke the truth. You were ready to sacrifice yourself to save my life. You are indeed the bravest beast of all. But then, I always said so."

❀ Lies ❀

Would you like to hear some lies? If you'll listen, I will tell. One day I saw two roast geese running in the sky. They ran fast, fast, with their feet up, and their backs down. A hammer floated down the river, and a frog sat on an ice floe and ate two wolves. This happened in July. Three peasants wanted to catch a hare. One was blind, the other mute, and the third lame. The blind peasant saw the hare, the mute one told the lame one about it, and the lame one caught it. Last year I traveled to a distant country just across the river where mosquitoes were as large as dogs and rode bareback on cats. The people in that country went sailing on land in ships. They sailed across fields and hills, over rye and corn, till they came to a high mountain, and there they drowned. A turtle chased a mouse, and a cow ran up on the roof and lay down to rest. And now it's time to open the window and let all the lies fly out.

Mirra Ginsburg

was born in a small town in Russia where, she says, "Despite the Revolution the life that gave birth to the folk tales and fables I now collect and translate was almost literally the life of my childhood."

After leaving Russia she lived with her family in Latvia, then Canada, and finally settled in New York City. A noted editor and anthologist who translates from both Russian and Yiddish, Miss Ginsburg has been gathering children's stories and folklore for a number of years. Recently she began to publish some of this material in various collections for young people. She is currently working on a selection of plays by the Russian dramatist Yevgeny Zamyatin and is planning to translate more children's books.

Anita Lobel

was born in Krakow, Poland, where she spent much of her early childhood. She attended school in Stockholm, Sweden, and came to the United States in 1952. In New York City she studied art at Pratt Institute.

Having lived close to peasant art as a child, Mrs. Lobel has always been interested in the decorative arts. She embroiders clothes whenever she can and designs needlepoint tapestries.

She and her husband, the author–artist Arnold Lobel, now live in Brooklyn, New York. They have two children, Adrianne and Adam.

Her many books include *Sven's Bridge, The Troll Music, The Seamstress of Salzburg,* which she wrote and illustrated, and *The Little Wooden Farmer* and *Indian Summer,* for which she did the pictures.

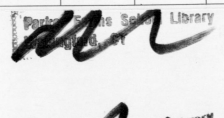